DISCOVER THIS UNIQUE COLLECTION OF COLORING PAGES

COLORING BOOKS

This is a Bleed Through Page If You Are Using a Colouring Marker or Pen!

Find Other Great Titles By searching for Bold Illustrations on Your Favorite Book Retailer

Amazon.Ca | Barnes & Noble (BN.Com) | Books A Million (BAM.Com)

This is a Bleed Through Page If You Are Using a Colouring Marker or Pen!
Find Other Great Titles By searching for Bold Illustrations on Your Favorite Book Retailer
Amazon.Ca | Barnes & Noble (BN.Com) | Books A Million (BAM.Com)

P

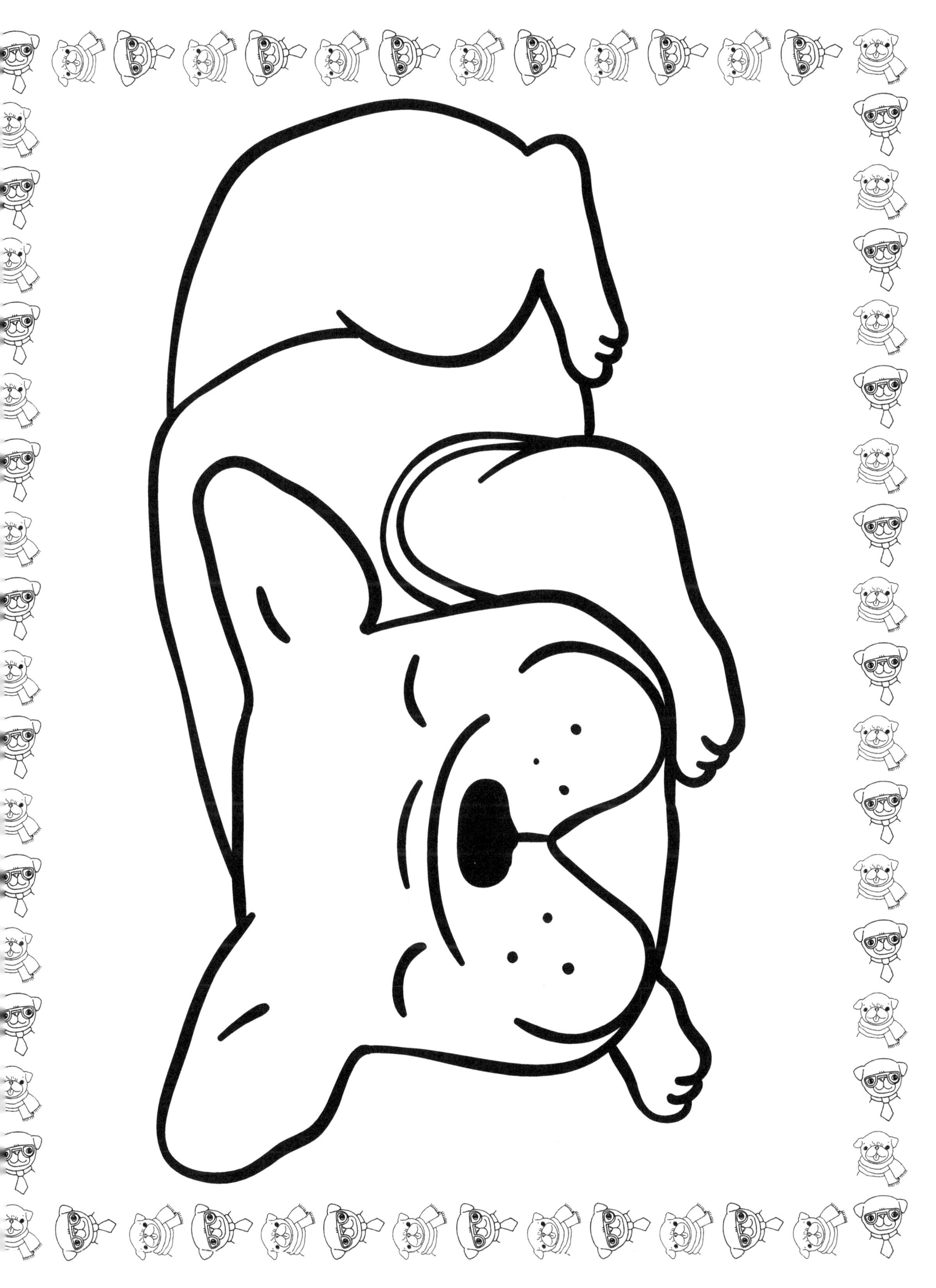

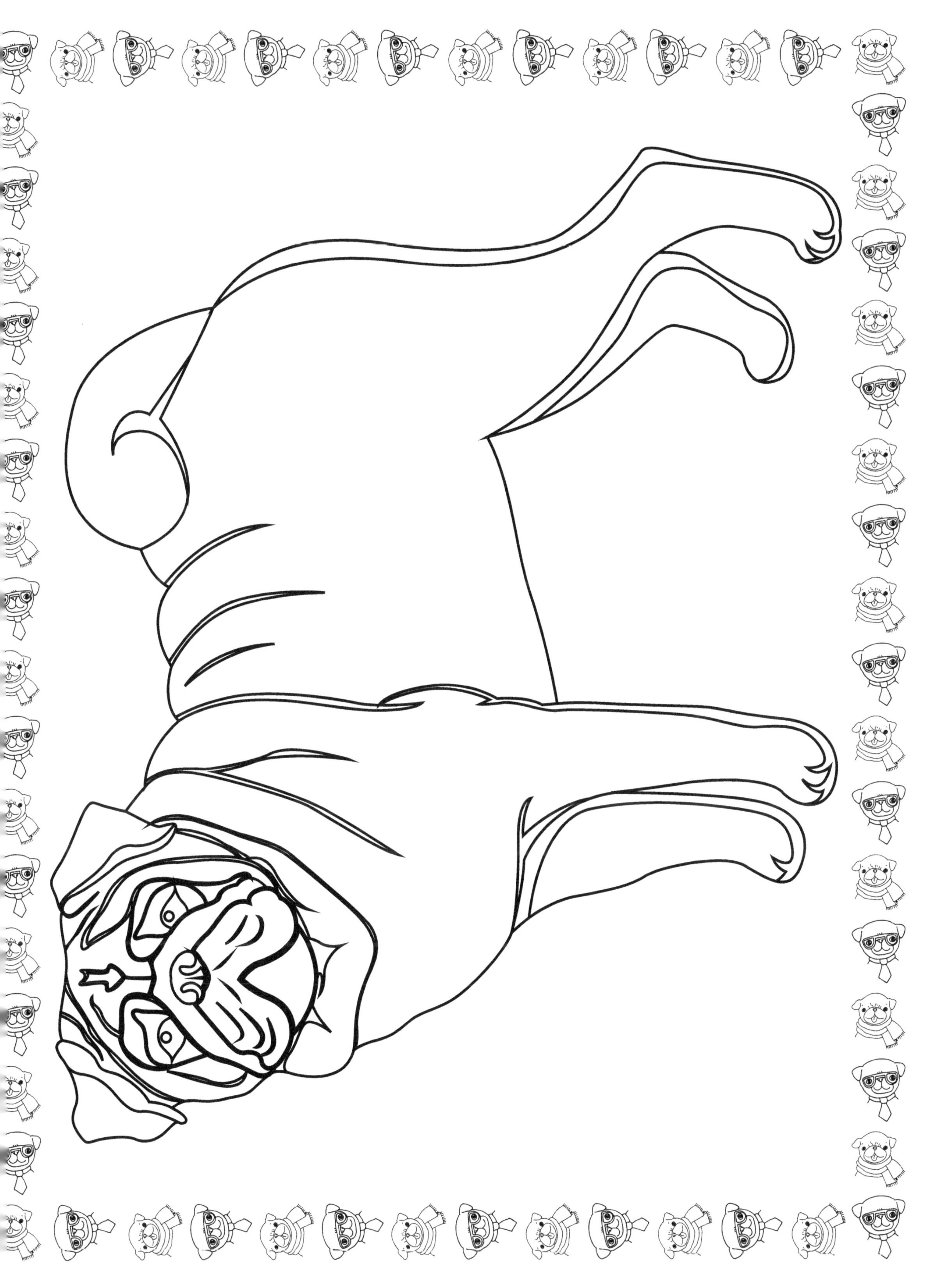

CPSIA information can be obtained
at www.ICGtesting.com
Printed in the USA
BVHW012156230320
575804BV00016B/305